TITLE

A HORRIBLE NIGHT

AUTHOR

FARHAN ILYAS

Chapter 1

At the point when Billy Hudson came shrieking into the sheriff's division the evening of August eighth, his cherry red Firebird came quite close to crashing into the valued Cadillac having a place with Sheriff Andrew Lutz.

At the point when he heard the screeching of tires, Sheriff Lutz turned upward from the obsolete magazine he had been absentmindedly browsing. He saw the bumper of Billy's Pontiac come swinging towards the driver's side entryway of his Caddy, and was out of his work area and part of the way through the station in one quick, smooth movement.

What the blasting damnation was Billy thinking, Lutz thought with a glance at his scraped metal watch. It was scarcely minutes into Saturday morning, and Lutz's first tendency was that the young fellow had been drinking. What sort of tipsy driver energetically drives himself into

police authority?

Before the wheels of the Firebird had come to a full stop, the driver's side entryway opened up and Billy Hudson tumbled out, tumbling to his knees previously staggering back to his feet.

"They're dead!" Billy yelled enthusiastically as he battled for balance. "The Mcguire's, I believe they're all

dead!"

Lutz's mouth was at that point open to reprimand Billy for almost crushing in the entryway of his Cadillac, yet at Billy's words his jaws snapped shut with a discernible snap. Lutz observed the scene before him.

He had been sheriff of Richmond County for more than a decade, having won re-appointment two times after Sheriff Bradley resigned back in '75. In a region with forty thousand occupants spread north of 400 square miles, he invested the majority of his energy in the parkways, thus was all around familiar with Billy Hudson and his gathering of gearheads. Billy was a courteous youngster, consistently deferential, however that wasn't generally the situation with the youngsters of the town.

The neighborhood adolescent young men were altogether fixated on their vehicles, and could frequently be tracked down on one desolate country street or another late around evening time, drinking and racing furthermore, having a by and large wild time. They weren't awful children essentially, there simply was very little else to do in a space that was on the whole surrendered to corn and soybean fields. Something like one time each month, Lutz or one of his agents would need to go out and scatter the gathering once they got excessively boisterous and started shooting the speakers on their sound systems adequately noisy to wake the forbearing ranchers nearby.

With a sinking heart, Lutz thought he realized what may have occurred. "Which one of you hit them? Where is the mishap?" he went after the walkie-talkie at his hip, however Billy shook his head passionately, "Nobody hit them sheriff. We weren't hustling this evening. Stu Lennox is in major trouble with his Daddy for destroying his pristine Passage and - - "

"Cut to the chase, Billy!" Lutz growed.

1

"Apologies, sir," Billy's started talking so rapidly his words stumbled more than each other as they hustled to get out, and he needed to take a full breath prior to proceeding. "Nobody was dashing this evening, Sheriff. I was out with Molly Greene, she lives over in Oakville. We went to the drive-in, and I brought her back home. Coming back I needed to - - I chose to take old Highway 99. I like how quiet it is out there around evening time."

Needed to upset the harmony by firing up the Pontiac away from the officers on the public parkway is more similar to it. Sheriff Lutz thought yet didn't voice out loud.

"At any rate, I was over by the McGuire place, you know that large fix of woods out by that ranch? I was driving out there and I- - I assumed I saw something cross the street. Like a dull shadow, greater than a bear. Frightened the poop out of me. I almost failed to keep a grip on the vehicle."

"There aren't any bears around here child." the sheriff

answered distrustfully, "Certain it was anything but a deer?"

"It wasn't no damn deer, sir. It moved like a feline, yet it was slouched and inclining like a bear. I just saw it for a second, yet it certainly wasn't any deer I at any point seen. It was taller than the top of my vehicle!"

What garbage was this? Lutz ran a hand through his dim, diminishing hair and peered down. It was then that he saw the blood scattering Billy's dusty workboots furthermore, the trims of his pants.

Backing gradually away from the young fellow, Lutz edged his right hand very nearer to the gun holstered at his hip. He started peering toward the red Pontiac for imprints and scratches, expecting this account of a creature was nothing more than confusion. Seeing as none, he turned cautiously back to the young fellow, keeping a separation of ten feet.

"OK, Billy. You have around twelve seconds to begin checking out before we begin to have an issue. Why is it true that you are saying that the McGuire's are dead? Whose blood is on your shoes, child?"

"I was attempting to tell you, Sheriff. I was driving out on old Thruway 99, and I saw this enormous cumbersome shape cross the street. I don't have the foggiest idea what it was sir, legit. Be that as it may, it scared me terrible enough that I damn close slipped out. At the point when I at long last got the vehicle halted on the shoulder, I glanced around, yet anything it was had vanished

into that fix of woods close to the McGuire plot.

"I calculated equivalent to you, sir, " Billy proceeded,

"Thought I was simply seeing things late around evening time. However at that point

in my headlights, I could see some somewhat fluid on the street. Like oil...except when I looked again it wasn't oil.

It was blood."

"Is it conceivable this creature or anything that you saw could have been injured?" the sheriff inquired.

"That is the main thing I thought as well, sheriff, and I jumped out of the vehicle and got my Winchester rifle out of the storage compartment. Figured I could basically put the unfortunate animal out of its wretchedness. Be that as it may, when I drew nearer to the blood on the street - - when I drew nearer, I- - " Billy began stammering, furthermore, maybe all the strength in his legs gave out. He sank nimbly to his knees, his oil-stained blue pants sinking into the delicate grass of the station's yard.

"Let it out, child. What did you see?" Lutz inquired. He was attempting to be patient however it was additionally basic that they get to the location of any crime as quick as could really be expected.

Billy took a profound, shaking breath. "An arm, sir. On the roadside, just past my front light, was a woman's arm. Ripped off at the elbow. It was all the while wearing - still wearing a wedding ring." At this Billy began shaking so seriously the sheriff figured he may be nearly having a seizure.

Chapter 2

He searched briefly, perplexed at the turn of occasions his beforehand quiet night had taken. Then, at that point, he crouched on his rump close to the shudder young fellow. Without much forethought, Lutz sniffed the air around Billy Hudson's head, nearly expecting the obvious whiff of bourbon or gin. Yet, there was nothing.

Lutz transformed and strolled once more into the sheriff's office. "Clarkson!" he howled for his senior appointee. After a second, Henry Clarkson's head popped out of his little office, "Sheriff?"

Thank heavens it was Clarkson on the job this evening.

Clarkson was a quiet and able official, phenomenal in tense circumstances. The main African-American on the force, Henry Clarkson had a roaring voice and a profound barrel chest that could be utilized to extraordinary impact on wild suspects, however he likewise had a coherent brain that ticked through each conceivable situation prior to taking any activity. Express gratitude toward God it isn't Miller, Lutz reconsidered, this time in alleviation that it wasn't his more youthful, jumpier agent sharing the station this evening.

"Is the cruiser gassed up? Great. Get the rifle and the shotgun and get a few electric lamps too. We're going out to Highway 99; something might have occurred over

at Bud McGuire's place."

An extra advantage, Clarkson followed orders without peppering him with many inquiries. The delegate gestured in no time, and went to do as inquired. In the interim, Lutz returned outside and hunched down close to Billy Hudson, who was all the while bowing on the yard, his head in his grasp. Lutz' mouth had a harsh taste and he yearned for a cigarette.

"It's alright, Billy. You accomplished something useful, child. It's alright. Just inhale," Andrew Lutz mumbled this reiteration over and over, recollecting as he did the way his own dad utilized a comparative procedure to quiet sketchy ponies. Sure enough, following a little while Billy Hudson's relaxing started to slow, and the inflexible strain along his spine loose. Billy took a couple of all the more sluggish, shaking breaths and gazed toward the sheriff.

"After I found the arm, I went into the house," he said with dreary determination. "I - I can't make sense of it, sir. However something - - awful occurred in there. I might want to go home currently please, assuming that is completely fine."

Sheriff Lutz needed to tell Billy Hudson that he could go home, have a hot shower and a solid beverage, it was not intended to be. "Apologies, Billy. We really want you to show us precisely where all of this occurred. There aren't any lights out there, we'll drive directly past it in obscurity."

A flash disregarded Billy's face, similar to he was stifling back tears, yet his jaw fixed and he just gave a short, miserable gesture.

Lutz called his lesser delegate at home, awakening him out of a profound lay down with requests to pull his butt over and man the station while the two senior men went to mind the Mcguire's.

Then, at that point, them three packed into the sheriff's cruiser also, traveled north to Highway 99.

The twenty miles from the sheriff's station to the McGuire ranch passed in practically complete quietness as the for the most part obscured structures of the modest community gave way to the altogether obscured farmland that made up ninety percent of the area. Vast sections of land of corn and soybeans outlined each modest community in the province, with up to forty miles between networks. Lutz had spent his whole life in Richmond district, and for him the skyline would continuously be where the sky met the fields.

This boundless breadth of developed land was intruded, once in a while, by patchy patches of trees and clean brush. The vast majority of these "woodlands" were scarcely twenty sections of landwide, aside from the Iowa River Nature Preserve, which spread over almost thirty miles of land on the western side of the interstate. On the eastern side of the street was Bud McGuire's ranch.

Those woods had consistently made Andrew Lutz feel uncomfortable.

It was an odd, quiet spot of skeletal pines and briar shrubs, offering none of the mystery trails and streaming floods of the patches of woods he had delighted in as a kid. It was likewise unused by trackers, even in a locale gagged with hungry deer they really wanted to bite on the extreme pine bark presented by the trees. No difference either way

"nature" the state government was determined to

"protecting" was an open inquiry.

The smallest bit of waxing moon sparkled overhead, not giving sufficient brightening to make out anything past the orange light emission cruiser's headlights.

Each man was lost in his viewpoints. Sheriff Lutz had passed the overgeneralized terms of the matter on to his representative as they had pulled out of the station. No less than one loss. Probable more. Reports of a huge creature. Conceivably a mountain lion.

"A mountain lion, sir?" Officer Clarkson had asked in complete bewilderment when Andrew had told him.

"Have you glanced around, Sheriff? You see any fucking mountains? On the off chance that we are going out to the Bud McGuire's house, sir, you know as well as I do what we're going out there to find."

Indeed. Lutz thought as he maneuvered onto the hollowed black-top of Expressway 99.

I know precisely exact thing we're probably going to find.

His hands tingled for a cigarette yet he pushed the desire aside. He permitted his contemplations to float to Bud McGuire also, attempted to overlook the premonition of fear in his stomach.

****

Andrew Lutz had been in his mid-twenties when he had first experienced Buddy McGuire. He had been out on watch one evening, driving down the tranquil roads of the town when he had seen a young man in an deserted parcel, crouching in the residue close to a canine. The canine was lying on its side. Worried that a cherished pet had been struck by a vehicle, Lutz had left and moved toward the pair.

The canine, a mottle mutt with wide, miserable eyes was writhing in the residue, gasping shallowly as the youthful kid watched. Pal could never have been more than eight or nine years of age at that point, however he showed not a glint of feeling as he watched the withering creature.

"Is this your canine, child?" Lutz had asked merciful.

Amigo hadn't replied. Most children were unfailingly pleasant to cops, as least back then, however Mate essentially overlooked Lutz and kept watching the canine as it's breathing turned out to be more slow.

"Do you have at least some idea what befell this creature?" Lutz attempted once more.

Chapter 3

As yet nothing. However at that point Lutz had seen a sheet of butcher's paper jumbled at the kid's feet. Looking closer, he could likewise see pieces of a ground of some sort or another meat. An image of what had happened here was starting to shape to him.

"Did you give harmed lure to this canine, kid!" Lutz requested, raising his voice interestingly.

At his yell, the kid at long last turned at met Lutz' eyes.

The vague, passive look on the substance of the kid made the official make a stride back in shock. There was no trepidation, no touch of terrorizing at being tended to by a more bizarre, a police officer at that. There was nothing reflecting back in Buddy McGuire's eyes.

Shaken, Lutz had revealed the episode to then-Sheriff Bradley. Bradley had guided his thumbs into the listing belt of his pants and called attention to that it had been a homeless creature, not an esteemed pet. It was a horrendous passing certainly, yet nearby ranchers frequently shot or harmed strays that meandered onto their properties.

The mutts would sporadically kill chickens, ducks, or indeed, even start threatening the rancher's youngsters as they played outside. It was a means to an end; one the kid had presumably gained from watching his own dad.

Lutz had returned to the unwanted parcel later that evening and covered the creature himself.

Throughout the following decade, Buddy McGuire made a name for himself as one of those young men who are very great at harming individuals. At the point when he was in 6th grade, an upperclassman had prodded Buddy about his messy, unkempt hair. In full perspective on the understudies and educators, Pal had strolled over to the more seasoned kid, got his wrist, and turned until bones crunched.

Bud McGuire had been ousted in 10th grade, and was with perfect timing to be cleared up by the Vietnam War two years after the fact. Nobody very understands what he got up to over there, yet when he got back to the town in '75, it was as on the off chance that a sweeping of fury had settled itself on Bud's shoulders.

His dad had passed on from disease while he had been sent, and Bud assumed control over his family's hundred or something like that sections of land. This little ranch was scarcely have been sufficient to keep food in their stomachs and garments on their backs, however it had been in the family for three ages.

The dirt, that thick dark Midwestern soil, bombed Bud McGuire. Corn, beans, wheat, each harvest he planted appeared to shrivel and bite the dust at his touch. His individual ranchers succeeded, the rich soil of the land growing solid lines areas of strength for of corn apparently for the time being.

Regardless of all of this, Bud some way or another figured out how to land

himself a spouse. In the fall of 1977, a simple fifteen months after Bud returned from the conflict, a pale slip of a young lady was seen draping clothing on the front grass of the McGuire ranch. She had long, drab earthy colored hair and wide blue eyes that were perpetually fixed on the ground. What her identity was, where she came from, was anybody's

surmise. This would have incensed the ladies of the local area, every one of whom were fixated on heredity, be that as it may, no data on the young lady could be found. She was just there one day, quietly taking care of chickens or beating mats. She never came into town. Never addressed anybody.

The second time Andrew Lutz experienced Bud McGuire in an expert limit had been about a year after the appearance of this baffling lady. The local people had surrendered in irritation; all of their good thoughts and housewarming meals had been met with a shut entryway. The McGuire's had never been seen going to any of the many places of worship in the local area, nor had the young lady showed up at the general store where the spouses could jump on her.

The underlying disarray had given approach to noble anger. Who did they assume they were, stayed all arrogant on their plot of land? Did the McGuires'

think they were too great to even consider partner with their friends?

In any case, as the weeks delayed despite everything there was no sight of the young lady around. Winter set in, and she was

as of now not seen external by the couple of individuals who drove on the old province street. The irritated sensations of the residents started to move into concern. Might it be said that she was alright?

All things considered, Buddy had consistently had an incredible attitude, even prior to his years in the wildernesses of Vietnam.

At long last, in the spring of '78 the spouses annoyed their spouses until the husbands had called the city police.

The police thusly, called the sheriff's specialty to tell them that somebody expected to go keep an eye on that young lady, to relieve the nerves of their stressed neighbors. Lutz had been the lesser representative on the job at that point, and had set off up Highway 99 to the McGuire ranch.

Scarcely three miles from the floodplains of the Mississippi River, the ground in March was an entanglement of mud that had sucked at Lutz' boots as he ventured out of the police cruiser. The house was a customary farmhouse, two stories with clearing peaks that rose to make a third story in the storage room. An enormous, wraparound yard maintained by thick wooden bars hinted at the entrance. Lutz had glanced around carefully previously climbing the steps to the yard. He had thumped two times.

No response. This had been normal, and Lutz turned away from the house and went rather around the back, where sure enough a unimposing young lady was arranging crisp spring spices into a variety of bowls.

She had seethed like a frightened feline when she got sight of him, and Lutz had held his hands before him to show he had only good intentions. "Good day, ma'am. I'm Representative Lutz, I'm with the sheriff's specialization. Can I ask your name?" he talked in a low, delicate voice, taking exceptionally sluggish strides towards the young lady.

The young lady's eyes had been sky-blue as they investigated his with an indiscernible articulation.

"April"

The word had been minimal more than a breathe out of breath, furthermore, Lutz had been going to request that she rehash the same thing at the point when the young lady's eyes had centered around something behind his shoulder and enlarged with alert.

Lutz had gone to see Bud McGuire standing a couple paces behind them. His bruised eyes had been similarly as clear and cruel as when he had looked at that passing on canine. Inclining with easygoing hazard on his shoulder, pointed at the sky, was a twofold barreled shotgun with a long, smooth gag.

Lutz had fortunately fought the temptation to alarm at the sight of the husky man. "Morning, Bud," he said. With slow purposeful developments, Lutz had moved his hand to the gun raised at his hip and thumbed open the catch.

Bud had seen, as he was intended to. His mouth bent in a glare, he had answered, "You're not wanted here,"

he had said in a level, tedious voice, and Lutz had understood this was whenever he first was hearing Bud talk.

Chapter 4

"I'll leave in practically no time," Lutz had answered in an legitimate tone. "Individuals have been thinking about how both of you have been getting on up here without help from anyone else all winter. Thought I'd come over and make sure that everything was okay."

"Fine. You've seen. Presently go," and with that, Bud had crossed the brief distance among him and his new spouse. Lutz had hung tight for him to hit her, assuming that he did than the appointee could carry him into the station, yet Bud just stood a couple of feet from the young lady with a look of unadulterated fierceness on

his face.

April McGuire had been completely quiet during this experience. Presently she sprang from her table of spices as though burnt. She stooped then, and Lutz saw something he hadn't seen previously. Under the table was an enormous wicker bin fixed with woolen covers. Settled resting in the covers was a little, wrapped up baby.

The young lady grabbed up the container and escaped into the house without another word. Bud had turned, the shotgun still adjusted on his shoulder. "This is my property. Ain't no

wrongdoing been carried out. You persuaded no option to be here." All of this was said in a similar shocking, empty voice.

Bud's words, expressed in a similar shocking, lifeless voice, were all evident. April McGuire had not blamed Bud for anything. It wasn't illegal to hold a gun

while remaining on your own territory. There was nothing something else for Lutz to say, so he had withdrawn back to the cruiser and gone to the station.

He hadn't gotten back to the McGuire property since that day almost a long time back. The McGuire's had been seen something like a small bunch of times in those eight years, most frequently driving in Bud's battered Dodge Ram as the family returned or drove away along Highway 99.

Sooner or later another kid, a girl, was added to their number. Neither one of the kids was at any point seen at the nearby state funded school or the neighborhood Christian school.

Commonly Lutz had driven gradually down the region street, wanting to see April McGuire or her kids out in the yard. Yet, the house had been covered and quiet, furthermore, Lutz had been compelled to continue to drive. Over the years, the majority of individuals locally had long since quit chattering about the McGuires. Everybody felt for the desolate young lady disconnected with her youngsters and Bud's resentment. Be that as it may, these were likewise a moderate gathering who valued their right to protection. As

long as there was no obvious issue at the McGuire ranch, everybody simply shook their heads and went about their lives, despite the fact that they all knew what the extreme result was probably going to be.

As Sheriff Andrew Lutz approached the McGuire estate, he was reviling himself for not accomplishing more, for not imagining a ludicrous motivation to go mind April also, her youngsters.

He just trusted he wasn't past the point of no return.

Yet, it didn't look like that were the situation.

"Uh, sir?" the voice of Billy Hudson out of nowhere snapped Andrew Lutz out of his responsibility and distress. Consumed by his evil considerations, he was going to miss the visually impaired bend in the street paving the way to Bud's ranch. The weighty police cruiser was rather pointed straightforwardly at an enormous pine tree.

Lutz curved the guiding wheel fiercely, and the massive vehicle shrieked its protection from such treatment, fishtailing fiercely across the street in lengthy, winding bends before he had the option to gain influence.

Heart pounding from the close to miss, the Sheriff pointed the vehicle at the shallow rock shoulder and pulled over. His hands were gripping the guiding wheel in a white-knuckle grasp, and it paused for a minute of work to deliver them. He killed the motor and for a long second the main sound was the calm ticking of the

motor as it cooled. In front of this bend, the trees would open on side toward the start of the McGuire ranch.

"Sorry about that folks," he at long last figured out how to say.

Official Clarkson was taking a gander at him with unadulterated shock, as though he had quite recently seen a mountain lion in the farmlands of Iowa. In the rearview reflect, Billy met his look with a dull look as the two officials unclipped their safety belts and ventured out into the moist summer night.

Right away, something felt off, and the tissue on Lutz'

arms crept. He motioned for Clarkson to go along with him, what's more, let Billy out of his enclosure in the secondary lounge.

Crossing to the storage compartment, Lutz took out the rifle and given it to Deputy Clarkson. He snatched the shotgun furthermore, two high-bar electric lamps prior to shutting the storage compartment.

With a gesture of understanding, he passed the shotgun and one of the electric lamps to Billy Hudson.

All of the young men and the majority of the young ladies around here figured out how to shoot before they were a decade old.

Information on guns and gun security was profoundly imbued locally where nearly everybody's

profound coolers were supplied loaded with new venison each pre-winter. Lutz felt no wavering about giving the shotgun over to the more youthful man. The youngster had sense, regardless of whether he was excessively enamored with racing.

His driver's side entryway was as yet open; Lutz came to in to switch off the headlights and afterward reconsidered. The faint light was all they had adjacent to the weighty Maglite he now conveyed inverse his administration gun. He left the cruiser's lights running, shut the way to the vehicle with a weighty crash, and them three went to overview their environmental factors.

That odd inclination was all the while crawling up the rear of Lutz'

neck, however it was Billy who had the option to give voice to his anxiety. "Every one of the bugs hush up," the young fellow murmured. Lutz listened cautiously and acknowledged he was right.

This was high summer, the air was thick and sticky and it ought to have been loaded up with the tweets of bugs. The daily concerto of katydids, cicadas, and crickets was typically enough to make a man half-frantic yet here there wasn't to such an extent as the buzz of a mosquito. The as it were sound was the tranquil tapping of the men's boots as they started strolling north towards Bud McGuire's home.

The light from the headlights didn't neglected to infiltrate the despair ahead, and Lutz tapped on the powerful Maglite. Close to him, Billy bore the shotgun, his more modest electric lamp squeezed with one hand under the barrel. Appointee Clarkson was primed and ready with the long Winchester rifle at his shoulder.

Chapter 5

Ordinarily utilized when a

representative expected to put down an injured creature on the side of the interstate, Lutz was enormously thankful just presently for it's positively dependable presence.

Lutz cleared the electric lamp in sluggish, cautious strokes from one edge of the way to another. "Where did you say you saw this arm now, child?" he asked Billy.

"Umm… somewhat farther ahead, I think," Billy's voice came from his right. "Perhaps another 300 feet or so."

Lutz proceeded with purposefully clearing his spotlight from one side to another. At the edge of the bar he could make out the consumed elastic made by tires out of nowhere sliding across the street. The tracks went on up the street, disappearing into the haziness.

The men were presently far enough away from the family member security of the vehicle that it's faint headlights could no more help with infiltrating the anguish ahead. The bars from the two electric lamps appeared to become more modest and fainter as the strolled in free arrangement up the street.

Unexpectedly, the consumed elastic pallet made by Billy's tires reached a conclusion around six feet before them. The three

men generally halted together, gazing dumbfoundedly ahead. In the light emission's electric lamp, on the edge of the street as it blurred into scour grass, was the arm of a human female. It had been torn roughly at the elbow, also, ridiculous strings of meat swung from one end. The opposite end was wearing a meager gold wedding ring around the ring finger. The nails were chipped and installed with soil.

All the blood in his body appeared to be race to his head, and Lutz could feel his pulse beating nauseatingly in his sanctuaries. Delegate Clarkson gave a fierce hurl and gone to upchuck discreetly into the trench on the opposite side of the roadway. Lutz crouched on his hindquarters close to the cut off arm, and went after the ballpoint pen he kept in his shirt pocket. Turning his head to take one more breath of unfouled air, he utilized the pen to lift one of the segments of tissue away from the injury. It had been practically destroyed, and for one astonishing moment the picture of Lutz' late spouse's venison jerky came to his mind. Acrid bile rose in his throat, and he battled against the inclination to vomit.

What creature could do this to an individual? What creature could irritate?

As far as anyone is concerned, there had never been a reports of bear around here, and any wolves had been killed off

ages back. Coyotes would take a chicken or a duck once in for some time, yet Lutz couldn't remember a solitary occasion of them pursuing a little youngster, not to mention a developed lady. Furthermore, these weren't the teeth or hook marks of a coyote. Whatever had done this had a lot longer teeth.

An unexpected snap from the woodland to his left side.

Lutz' blood went to ice in his veins. Clarkson heard it as well. His rifle was once again at his shoulder in a moment and he made a reluctant stride towards the approaching darkness.

Close to him, Billy Hudson was absolutely inflexible, his fingers dreadful white around the hold of the shotgun.

One more snap in the murkiness. Had that one been nearer?

He immediately swung the light emission spotlight away from the frightful scene out and about, toward the woods. It enlightened skeletal pine trees and midriff high thornbushes. The light sparkled frightfully on the limited trunks of the pines. With their stepping stools of broken branches, the trees became columns of threatening lances standing by to pierce unwary voyagers. The unnatural quietness of the forest was harsh.

Lutz looked into the obscurity, willing the shadows to separate into shapes. He zeroed in on the edges of the light, where it blurred into a thick and impervious darkness. He figured he could see shapes in obscurity,

approaching patches of shadow that were some way or another more black than the evening. A huge figure moving barely out of his field of vision.

Yet, nothing came charging at them from out of the woods, and after a long second Lutz loosened up his pose. Telling himself unconvincingly that it had been a deer, Lutz turned around to Billy. They currently had proof of a demise, yet not be guaranteed to proof of a wrongdoing. There was still work to be finished before they could all return home. "Did you say there were something else bodies?" he inquired.

Billy delayed the slightest bit and afterward answered, "Yes.

Perhaps? I don't have any idea. Just… just come see for yourselves."

Clarkson looked confounded by the response, yet entirely rolled his eyes and shrugged, "How about we finish this, Sheriff. This place gives me the fucking creeps."

Hearing his agent concede his anxiety some way or another effectively helped Lutz' own certainty. The woods was presently at his back, and he felt full concentrations eyes on them yet he shook off his nerves. Gesturing confirmation at Billy, he affirmed, "How about we get this the fuck over with and go home."

Leaving the solitary, desolate arm on the thruway, the men currently started avoiding the edge of the cornfield

that lined Bud McGuire's home. The corn, which ought to have overshadowed them at a full level of sixteen feet, was debilitated looking and skinny. This as a matter of fact offered Lutz some solace, the debilitated stalks of the malnourished harvests made it simpler for the bar of his Maglite to penetrate the fields.

Approaching ahead, put off almost a quarter mile from the edge of the parkway, was the McGuire house. From the outset, it looked similarly as when Lutz had paid his visit eight years already, yet the decay of the home turned out to be progressively evident as they turned onto the free rock carport.

Toward the beginning of the way was a rust-eaten post box, inclining dubiously on its endured wooden post. The McGuire's had clearly neglected to stay aware of their correspondence. He pondered inactively how Bud took care of things like power and plumbing if charges never came to their home.

The fundamental house probably been genuinely exquisite in some time long since past. It's casing was a perfect and fresh Colonial, with gabled windows and a huge fold over patio.

However, the perfect lines were darkened by a hanging rooftop and missing screens. The patio was likewise hanging, with a feeble wicker sofa sitting failed to one

Corner.

Chapter 6

What should whenever have been happy white paint furthermore, blue managing was presently dark and stripping in perfect takes from the wood. The entire house had a quality of weariness, similar to a once-glad old pony that no more had the energy to hold its head up in the follows.

The front entryway was hanging open by one contorted pivot.

As the men moved toward Lutz held up one hand twisted into a clench hand as a sign to hold position.His prior butterflies had cleaned up, supplanted by the inquisitively segregated feeling he generally felt while was moving toward a wrongdoing scene that sure to be undesirable. Typically it was a high school kid who celebrated too hard and wrapped his vehicle around a tree. Or on the other hand a driver who got back home alcoholic and chosen to place his better half in the funeral home. Following thirty years in the sheriff's area of expertise, Lutz was no more peculiar to the savagery intrinsic in men.

However, it was anything but a man that detached that youngster's arm.

As though to affirm this chilling idea, Lutz sparkled his electric lamp on the wrecked entryway of the house. Scratched profound into the wood, profound enough that the entryway was almost fragmented into pieces, were four equal gouges running from the highest point of the door jamb to the base

corner in one long, solid curve. The aluminum door handle was wound rusty and hung pointlessly aside.

Past the entryway lay just more obscurity.

Delegate Clarkson had been a superbly decent game up until this point, yet when given the possibility of passing the boundary of this house, he recoiled. He delivered his stranglehold on his rifle, bringing it down to his side and shouting, "No offense, Sheriff, yet to hell with this.

I'm not goin' in there. We should return to the vehicle and call- -

"Call who, Henry?" Lutz said straight. "The state officers can do nothing with the exception of compose passes to tourists.

The town police consider us when there is a vicious demise. So who precisely would it be a good idea for us to call? Creature control?"

Clarkson glared back at him, "Then we should return to the vehicle and return the goddamn light, " he murmured between ground teeth.

By and by, Lutz felt that Clarkson was talking the most sense that anybody had throughout the evening. In any case, as much as he secretly concurred with his delegate's arrangement to withdraw far away from the McGuire house, they were there and there was something important to take care of. "Come on now, Henry. Billy's been inside. Can't allow the youngster to show us up now, can we?" Lutz said with a constrained good cheer that rang bogus in his ears.

He murmured, ran one hand along his temple and through his salt-and-pepper hair, and attempted once more. "Better believe it, this sucks. Doesn't change realities. We need to figure out what, if anything, happened here this evening. So how about we simply sack up and make it happen, is that right?"

It was a sorry motivational speech yet it appeared to do the stunt. Billy gave a weighty shrug, scraping his boots against the earthy colored grass lining the McGuire's entryway patio.

Clarkson shut his eyes briefly as though presenting a quiet petition, then reshouldered his gun and gestured at Lutz. "I'm requiring a long end of the week," he expressed matterof-factly.

"Going to take my better half up to Iowa City. Going to go to Red Lobster. It's Crabfest." He murmured to himself about his forthcoming end of the week, yet entirely brushed past Lutz and climbed the squeaking strides onto the patio.

You can have the entire week off. Lutz intellectually guaranteed his appointee. Then, at that point, he hauled his gun out of its holster, thumbed the security off, and followed the two men past the entry and into Bud McGuire's home.

A significant quietness settled around the men as they passed the boundary of the McGuire house. The strides made by the official's weighty boots were suppressed by the layer of residue that lay upon the floor. In the light emission spotlight, the backdrop in the anteroom may have been a radiant striped yellow sooner or later, be that as it may, had been distorted with water harm and was presently

the shade of old pee.

In front of the men was a long passage with an entryway on one or the other side. On one side, Lutz could see the omnipresent farmhouse "mudroom", complete with columns of elastic Wellington boots and weighty winter parkas.

The Wellies were dull and broken with neglect, and the coats were neglected and possessed a scent like moist. A shut entryway drove further into the house, likely into the kitchen.

On the left half of the hallway was a room Lutz' spouse would have alluded to as a "parlor" when she was alive, with fragile furnishings and arranged porcelain puppets. Here was the primary proof of human movement.

The petite tables were crushed to bits, and the rose-designed loveseat was at a characterized point to a motheaten mat, as though somebody had effectively moved the lounge chair by remaining with abrupt power. A wrecked water container lay in pieces on the floor.

Strangely, even these brutal scene was gentled by a thick layer of residue. Up to this point, the main sign that a living individual had been in the house were the tracks he could find in the hall that had plainly been made by Billy's weighty workboots.

Where could the Mcguire's have been's?

Lutz continued on a steady turn, sparkling his highpowered spotlight into each corner and cleft. His

faculties felt jolted as he stressed every last one of his faculties to decide if a danger actually snuck in this house. As per his eyes and ears, this was simply a typical house, however horrendously dismissed. "Billy,"

he murmured softly. "Why the fuck did you indeed, even come in here?"

Billy answered similarly discreetly, "Similar to I said, sir, I thought perhaps somebody was in a difficult situation. However, when I got here - - it was like I just needed to continue onward. I needed to see for myself."

Lutz got it. He could feel it as well. The panicky inclination to set out back toward the vehicle was muffled by dismal assurance. He expected to figure out what on God's green earth had occurred here.

Past the open entryways to the mudroom and the parlor was a stairway that went from the first floor the entire way to the storage room in a long bend. The steps, similar to all the other things in the McGuire house, appeared to be standing upstanding by sheer power of will alone.

Running along the right edge of the flight of stairs, in a long whole line start to finish, was a wide area of dried blood.

The primary idea that went through Sheriff Lutz' mind in that second was that he wished he lived in a bigger

city, with additional assets. In the event that they were farther north, close to Des Moines or Cedar Rapids, the three men remaining in the McGuire house could be encircled by reinforcement soon.

Chapter 7

A little armada of criminal investigators, criminological specialists, picture takers, proof baggers and rubberneckers could accumulate at the residence. The living haziness of the August summer night would be beaten back by powerful flashbulbs and battery-controlled spotlights. Under their cruel glare, and calmed by the shop discussion of the accumulated authorities, anything that repulsions had visited the McGuire family would be uncovered as another crime location, still grievous yet adequate to the mind. A normal grouping of occasions. Tragically, his little pocket of eastern Iowa was little and underpopulated, the specialists expected to appropriately research a potential wrongdoing were basically not set up.

However much Lutz feared the thought, it would need to be him that wandered up those steps, and it would need to be presently. He would need to wander up there, thus would Clarkson, as division guidelines precluded an official from entering a potential crime location alone.

Also, he needed Clarkson's consistent presence close to him with the Winchester.

That didn't mean they all needed to go. "Billy," Lutz said to the young fellow without turning, "to go up there a subsequent time, presently is your opportunity. Go sit tight for us on the patio. Stand watch."

"With all due regard sir, it is absolutely impossible that I am remaining down here without anyone else." Billy squared his shoulders and gave Lutz a disobedient look.

"Your decision, kid." Lutz gave him a gesture and turned around to the issue of the flight of stairs. They would need to ensure they didn't taint the crime location with their boots. The blood was thick every one of the down the steps, where it suddenly halted on the second to last riser.

Here, a somewhat thicker pool of blood actually sparkled with faint wetness under his spotlight.

Whatever had occurred here, had happened as of late.

"Without rushing gets it done, presently. Try not to step in it."

Pressing his thin casing to the furthest edge of the flight of stairs, Lutz put a weighty boot on the primary riser. A puff up dust emerged, and the step gave a wheezing moan, however it didn't clasp under his weight.

Lutz started gradually propelling his direction up the steps, squeezing immovably on every step first to test its dependability. The flight of stairs squeaked and groaned yet kept on holding

firm, and he motioned for Clarkson to follow. Lutz could hear his normally withdrawn appointee mumbling different supplications and swear words faintly.

The area of blood went on up the steps in an solid streak. Presently it drifted off to one side and vanished into the obscurity of a long hall. The overpowering smell was of soil and shape, yet the coppery smell of new blood was likewise thick in the air. A few outlined photographs hung at lopsided spans, their subjects totally clouded with dust. The residue on the floor was upset now, yet there were no unmistakable tracks; it had been tidied practically up away in a few spots.

Surrendered now to owning this, Lutz felt his prior dread retreat to the rear of his psyche. The adrenaline siphoning through his framework was working for him now, honing his concentration and steadying his heartbeat. The passageway opened two times to one side, and Lutz surrounded watchfully around the open access to the primary room.

A quick look uncovered a soiled washroom. Or then again maybe it had once been a washroom. Presently it was a load of stained and broken porcelain, with a rusted out pipe hanging freely where a sink might have been. Torn tile covered pieces of the floor, yet its vast majority was similar endured wood planks as the remainder of the

higher up. The air was weighty with the scents of flat grime and mold.

The way of blood, which had become thicker as they high level along the hall, went on down the corridor to the subsequent room. Lutz motioned toward Billy to cover the entry of the restroom, then he and Clarkson progressed, guns positioned and prepared. Lutz still conveyed the Maglite, held to the highest point of his administration gun, so he was quick to warily peer around the corner of the room toward the finish of the lobby.

At the point when Lutz initial sparkled his electric lamp into the obscured room, he really inhaled a murmur of alleviation. He had expected to find the flung and eviscerated groups of April M.

Clarkson confronted him, his ordinarily tranquil face a veil of strain and dread, "No doubt, how did that arm even get out there? For what reason does it seem as though nobody has lived here in five years? Where in the world are the McGuires!" this last sentence he said in a murmured yell.

"Might it be said that they are in the stable? The cellar? Sprouted cleave them up and convey them into the forest? Was it even Bud? What on earth were those paw blemishes on the entryway, Sheriff?" Clarkson proceeded with his scrutinizing in a voice that didn't cover his rising dread.

Lutz grasped his agent firmly by the shoulders, his

own trepidation gone notwithstanding his official's inexorably alarm, "obviously it was Bud, Henry. We'll track down him.

Sit back and relax." This thought, however terrible as it seemed to be, offered a sort of horrible solace. Bud McGuire may be a disturbed lunatic who had quite recently killed his whole family, yet he was a man.

A man drained when you shot him.

This entire time Billy Hudson had been quiet, his eyes fixed on the open entryway to the dirty washroom. Presently Billy made a sound as if to speak, and timidly said,

"Sheriff? You should see this."

Had there at any point been less welcome word's in human history? Lutz squeezed his nose between two fingers and hesitantly inquired, "What is it?"

Billy just signaled with the top of the shotgun, and in the splendid shine from his Maglite Lutz could see a slim line of blood gradually advancing from behind the open restroom entryway.

Promptly his heart, which had quite recently started to continue its consistently booked beat, began drilling ridiculously in his chest. Some way or another, at that time, Lutz knew.

Anything that they had come here to find was on the other side of that entryway.

Chapter 8

On their first walkthrough of the passageway, every one of the three men had been distracted by the way of blood that prompted the room toward the finish of the lobby. Presently, upon closer assessment, Lutz understood that there was the slightest flicker of light coming from the obscured restroom.

His mouth was extremely dry, and Lutz gulped hard and afterward, gun still good to go, he facilitated around the entryway of the washroom and set his back against the closest wall. He actually look at the corner and, tracking down it void, continued to circle gradually around the room.

Clarkson covered him from behind, while Billy stood Yet again monitor outside the room.

The light was coming from two gleaming candles, the tall glass ones of the sort his grandma used to consume on Sundays. The flares were faltering their last breaths, and two additional candles had proactively suffocated in their own wax. How long do those candles consume? Lutz given careful consideration to check and kept his eyes on a turn, attempting to see however much as could reasonably be expected about the scene.

The candles had been organized close to a chipped green bath. The framed a little circle, in

which was a darkened circle, as somebody had stupidly chosen to fabricate a fire in the floor.

On the edge of the bath was a hung a blurred calico dress. Lutz moved toward the article of clothing, which had been painstakingly organized so as not to wrinkle against the sides of the tub. The actual tub was unfilled.

Lutz unexpectedly froze as he heard Clarkson swore a low vow behind him. Loaded up with unexpected fear, he turned instinctually on his heel and ready to fire.

Interestingly that evening, Andrew Lutz shouted at the highest point of his lungs.

Drooped in one corner of the destroyed washroom, in a gradually spreading pool of blood, stayed of Bud McGuire.

Lutz couldn't tear his eyes from the abhorrent sight.

Bud McGuire's face was frozen in a quiet scream, wide eyes fixed unblinking at the roof. His chest had been torn open roughly. The flickering white of ribs jabbed through the slaughter.

Bud's legs were bowed at a unimaginable point to his middle.

He had been torn practically in two at the crotch.

The principal shout that passed Sheriff Lutz' lips was immediately followed by a second. He fell in reverse to the ground and landed hard on his back, utilizing the heels

of his feet to drive himself away from the mangled body. His back squeezed against the rusted green bath, and he inactively saw that the calico dress lain across the edge had a weak example of purple violets.

Then, at that point's, major areas of strength for Clarkson hands were wrapped around his own, and his appointee pulled Lutz to his feet.

They left the messed up washroom and its shocking items furthermore, went into the hallway, where Billy Hudson was currently mostly down the steps prompting the first floor.

The old flight of stairs squeaked compromising underneath their boots as the two officials followed the more youthful man first floor, frantic to move as fair away from Bud McGuire's disfigured cadaver as could really be expected.

Lutz burst out still-open front entryway and staggered down the patio steps. The moist summer air was like a relieving analgesic against his skin. His lungs hurled with the work to attract new breath and he sank to his knees, digging his clench hands into the hard rock of the walkway. He could hear the strides of Deputy Clarkson and Billy sounding down the steps and out onto the front yard.

They remained benevolently quiet as Lutz battled against the influxes of intensity and chills that continued to substitute their way through his veins. Remotely, as though noticing

another person from far above, Lutz figured out that he was having a fit of anxiety. With shaking arms he moved his weight until he was perched on the yard lining the front way. Dry grass popped as he brought his knees up to his brow and stayed there, taking in the night air. Some place close by a cricket trilled, breaking the quietness.

Crickets were all the while trilling.

Some way or another, this was an uplifting thought. Lutz raised his head and searched for a second at the night sky. The sun was still hours from rising and the sky was completely dark, aside from the a huge number of sparkling stars.

Lutz took a full breath and held it briefly before leisurely breathing out. He rehashed this consistent breathing two times more then, at that point, tediously got to his feet, recoiling as the two his knees broke in fight. He dismissed dry grass the jeans of his uniform and seen his mates, both of whom had remained

quietly close by this whole time.

Gesturing once in quiet appreciation, Lutz continued his authority as sheriff. Not a solitary one of them would express a word of his brief breakdown, however they could all vibe a unexpected change in the air, as though an unexpected obligation of family relationship had quite recently been produced. Lutz knew that the three of them would always be limited by the occasions of this

night.

Official Clarkson focused on his senior official. "Do you need to actually look at the remainder of the property? Search for the rest of the family?"

Lutz started shaking his head very quickly. "No, we found what we were searching for. This is formally a crime location. It's likewise a forty section of land ranch with two horse shelters what's more, no less than ten storehouses. We really want more men."

"You need to bring in Miller and Sanchez?" Clarkson inquired.

Lutz gestured, however at that point shook his head, "No doubt, we'll call them in when we return to the station. No radio transmission At any rate, over here good for anything. Moreover, I think we too need to get on the telephone with the city hall leader's office. We're going to require the legal sciences individuals in Iowa City or Davenport or any place the damnation."

At this, Sheriff Lutz turned and started strolling back the way they had come. Yet again he looked back at the obscured windows of the McGuire farmhouse, which presently seemed like approaching eyes in the retreating light from their spotlights. His boots crunched under the unpleasant rock of the long carport as the three men headed back towards the vehicle.

Chapter 9

The yellow, wiped out looking corn obstructed their view on either side, approaching far taller than a man even in this unfortunate state. Lutz was struck again by the spooky quiet of the spot. The muggy summer air was weighty nevertheless, not a breath of wind stirred through the stalks.

The close total shortfall of sound made him restless what's more, awkward. The sooner they were back to the vehicle the better.

Billy probably felt the same way; he jogged up close by Lutz, his rifle approximately got a handle on in one hand now that they were out of the farmhouse. In a soft tone he said, "What will happen now, Sheriff?"

Lutz shrugged, "First, we will return to the station. I have a container of Lagavulin 16 in a secured box my office. Sheriff Bradley gave me that bottle the day I got to work. Presently, he let me know this whisky was peaty enough and smoky enough to consume with extreme heat just horrible evening of your life.Told me there would some time or another come the night when I would require it. It's sat in it's wooden

box consistently until I truly began to feel that day could never come. In any case, come it did, and this evening I'm going to open that container and drink profound. Also, you'll drink with me, assuming you like."

Encouraged by this possibility, the men hurried up furthermore, inside a couple of moments they rose up out of the McGuire's carport back onto the smooth cleared surface of Highway 99. Like a heavenly messenger in the dimness, Lutz could see the police cruiser sitting on the edge of the street around 300 yards down. He relaxed a moan of help, understanding that some mystery part of him had expected the high contrast Chevy to be gone, leaving them abandoned at the McGuire ranch.

Lutz' palms were perspiring, and he cleaned them subtly on the thighs of his pants. He really look at his watch, then, at that point, really taken a look at it again in dismay. They had scarcely been gone forty minutes.

At the point when they arrived at the vehicle, Lutz' bobbled in his pocket for his keys, then, at that point, opened the entryway and slid into the driver's seat. His hands shuddered on the controlling wheel, what's more, he contemplated whether he was fit to drive.

Can't precisely request that Clarkson or Billy escort me home.

He thought resignedly. Lutz opened the traveler and indirect accesses, and his friends slid quietly into their seats. Clarkson was all the while holding the buck rifle, and the

shotgun was in Billy's lap, the mounted electric lamp still radiating a brilliant circle on the vehicle's upholstery. As one, the men secured their safety belts. The natural, regular snap of the metal sliding into place struck him as absolutely ludicrous after the night's occasions.

Lutz slid the way in to the Chevy into the start. He had a terrible, creeping feeling in the lower part of his stomach that when he turned the key, the motor would essentially decline to begin. This was absurd since the cruiser was scarcely three years of age and had sat idle yet murmur like a little cat. In any case, this evening, at the present time, the vehicle wouldn't begin. Since it couldn't be this simple to drive away.

The key turned, and the engine thundered to life, similarly as it continuously did. The front headlights came on, projecting two wide light emissions into the obscurity around them.

Reflecting back, inconceivably high against the skeletal pines of the woods, were a couple of sparkling red eyes.

Clarkson shouted first, tossing his hands over his face and shouting out in fear.

Lutz couldn't shout, his voice appeared to have totally locked itself away. His mouth expanded open in loathsomeness, however the main sound that came out was a choked stifle.

Billy was scrambling to escape the police cruiser, yet

since he was in the back the entryways just opened from the outside. He had a go at lowering the window, and when that bombed he started to overreact and slammed at the glass with his clench hand over and over, however this was similarly incapable.

Billy raised the knob of the shotgun and moved back, getting ready to smash it through the window of the vehicle.

"NO!" Lutz thundered, never taking his eyes from the shining red spheres watching them from the timberland.

He stuck the grasp in, appealing to anybody who may be listening that the vehicle didn't slow down. He moved into in the first place, gave the motor a few gas, and the vehicle started gradually moving. This whole time he gazed at the red eyes drifting twenty feet above them. They thought back steadfastly, sparkling with a malignant knowledge. As the cruiser moved past, the eyes followed their advancement, yet didn't progress. Lutz fixed his look on the rearview reflect, sitting tight for some covetous monster to come charging behind them.

Be that as it may, there was nothing. The murkiness of the night took over, and the eyes subsided into the trees.

Expectation presently on putting as much distance between himself and the McGuire ranch as could be expected, Lutz laid one weighty boot on the gas. Solely after ten miles, when he could see the lights of Harry Gibson's fuel station, did he

dial down his boot the gas pedal and unwind the slouched position of his shoulders. After ten minutes they pulled up to the obscured windows of the sheriff's station.

Lutz killed the driving force of the cruiser and the three men sat peacefully. After a long second, Henry Clarkson opened his mouth, "What was that thing - - " he started, however, Lutz set up available and halted him. Lutz shook his head, opened the entryway of the cruiser with a boisterous squeak, and ventured outside.

Each muscle in his body was blaming him for gross offense, and Lutz realized he would feel the discipline the following day. He opened the way to the sheriff's office and went in.

The agreeable environmental elements of the dirty sheriff's station nearly carried him to tears. Feebly humming security fluorescents cast a faint, yellowish shine on the natural chaos of work areas and seats. Without irritating to turn on the primary lights, he crossed the warm up area to the corner office at the rear of the station and headed inside his office. On the bookshelf against the far wall was a restricted wooden box, which Lutz currently opened for the first time in quite a while.

Settled against dull silk was the container of Lagavulin 16, given to him by resigning Sheriff Bradley on his last day in office.

There will come a day when you really want it.

Lutz motioned to Clarkson and Billy, who had followed him into the station and presently stood quietly behind him, outlining the way to his office. Clarkson had gotten three glasses from the little kitchen, and he set them down cautiously on the finished wood of Lutz' work area.

Andrew Lutz sat vigorously in his dark office seat. He bent the cap off the jug of scotch and poured three fingers into each glass. The golden fluid gleamed bluntly in the faint light.

The strong, peaty smell of the liquor

bit into his nose as he raised his glass and the two men before him raised theirs.

"Drink up," he prompted. In the one smooth movement all three of them depleted their glasses.

The scotch pioneered a red hot path to his stomach.

To consume the bad dreams with smoldering heat.

He came to top off his glass.

Thanks for reading

THE END

***

Document Outline